Joe in the Lions' Den

Helen Davie

Illustrated by Nick Ward

Scripture Union

Copyright © Helen Davie 2002

First published 2002

Scripture Union, 207–209 Queensway, Bletchley, Milton Keynes, MK2 2EB, England.
Email: info@scriptureunion.org.uk

Website: www.scriptureunion.org.uk

ISBN 1 85999 618 3

British Library Cataloguing-in-Publication Data.

A catalogue record of this book is available from the British Library.

Printed and bound in Great Britain by Creative Print and Design (Wales) Ebbw Vale.

Scripture Union is an international Christian charity working with churches in more than 130 countries, providing resources to bring the good news about Jesus Christ to children, young people and families and to encourage them to develop spiritually through the Bible and prayer.

As well as our network of volunteers, staff and associates who run holidays, church-based events and school Christian groups, we produce a wide range of publications and support those who use our resources through training programmes.

For Margaret and Jim Lacy, my parents.

Chapter 1

Joe was so mad he saw red.

"Get out of my room, Em!" he yelled.

Ever since Joe had got up, people had been pestering him.

"Please, Joe, help me with my Lego helicopter. I'm stuck," begged his little brother, Rob. Rob was a bit young for the Lego kit. It had 'Age 8' on it and Rob was only six. Joe had helped him with it before, but this morning, this particular wonderful free Saturday morning, he just didn't want to. He had plans!

Mum cooked a special Saturday breakfast with eggs, bacon, sausage, baked beans and fried bread. Things seemed to be looking up. Then Joe heard the postbox clatter.

"My *Beano*!" he thought.

Quick as lightning he took a great leap out of his chair to get to the comic before his sister, Em. ('Em' was short for Emma.) It was almost in his hand when...

"Please wash the mugs, Joe," said Mum, still cooking.

It was fatal. Joe hesitated, and in that fraction of a second, Em grabbed the comic. She smirked.

"It's not fair! It's mine!" shouted Joe.

Mum looked round.

"Well, she can read it while you wash the mugs," she said.

"I don't want to wash up on Saturday!" said Joe. "And it's Em's turn!"

"I have to cook for you on Saturday," said Mum. "Whoops!"

Joe's baby brother Alex was waving his spoonful of egg madly about. Mum reached over to take the spoon from Alex's hand. Joe muttered and slowly started on the dishes.

"By the way, Joe," said Dad, "you need new school shoes. We must go to town."

Joe's heart sank. Bye-bye lovely Saturday.

At last the washing up was done. Joe had managed to get the *Beano* back. Rob had gone out to play. Dad had remembered he'd promised to help his friend dig over his allotment today. He had decided to buy Joe's shoes another day. Mum was busy washing most of Alex's breakfast off him. Nobody was telling Joe to do anything.

Peace! Joe escaped upstairs, flopped down on his bed and stared at the wall. There on the shelf was the magnetic chess set Sam had given him for his birthday. Sam had been his best friend but Sam's dad had been given a job somewhere else and Sam had moved away. If Sam had been here Joe could have gone to his house and played with him.

Oh well! Joe picked up the *Beano* and started on the first cartoon, 'Dennis the Menace'.

Then in came Em, carrying her school books.

"I want to use the computer," she said. "I need to do my homework. Mum will let me."

She fixed Joe, who was nine, with a superior eleven-year-old glare.

"Oh no!" wailed Joe. He knew Em was right. He had the biggest bedroom so he had the computer. Now that Em was in the top class at school, she did get homework. Mum was very keen on that sort of thing.

"Well I'm going out, then. Get out while I get dressed properly. You'll just have to wait," he said.

He took as long as he could about it. In ten minutes Em was banging on the door. In eleven minutes she was yelling. In eleven and a half minutes Mum was getting cross, too.

Joe opened the door, comic in hand.

"I'm all ready," he told them, walking slowly past. Then he leaped for the stairs and shot out of the front door with relief. Now the main business of the day could begin!

Outside, Joe turned left and made for the copse at the end of the road. It backed on to the hedge that ringed the allotments. There, in a hollow between some scrubby trees and the hedge, Joe was building a den. He had stuffed some branches in the gaps at the base of the trees around the hollow to make a low wall. Then he'd carefully covered them with bracken and leaves. As the hollow was quite deep, he couldn't be seen unless someone came right up to it. It was a good den.

I've got to get the walls higher and make a decent roof, thought Joe.

He crawled in and sat down, looking at the two planks he'd wedged over his head. They didn't keep much rain off. But at least the den was secret and just his! After he'd read his *Beano* he'd have another hunt for building materials.

An hour later he was on his tummy, squashing his hand through the allotment fence. He could nearly reach that nice long bit of thin planking. He was just grasping it when it was suddenly whisked away.

"Oy, I need that!" grumbled a voice. "What d'you think you're doing?"

Joe's face was squashed against the fence. He screwed his head sideways and looked up. An old man in wellies with a brown, lined face and a floppy hat looked down at him.

"Sorry, I didn't know," puffed Joe. He wriggled backwards, scratching his arm as he pulled it out.

"I know you. I've seen you in church," said the man. "That's your dad over there, isn't it?"

Oh, no, sure enough, there was Dad, digging away in his friend Chris' allotment. If this man told Dad that Joe had tried to pinch something, that would mean trouble.

"I won't say anything," decided the man, "but you know better. Go on, get on your way."

"Thanks," breathed Joe. He ran off before

the man changed his mind. Dad wouldn't be pleased, even if it was only a bit of old plank.

Joe found some long branches, dragged them back and wedged them across the den. They stuck out a bit. If only he had a good knife to trim them off with. It looked more like a roof, though it probably still wouldn't keep much rain off. He gave up and went home for lunch.

It was a good lunch. Mum cooked yummy fluffy omelettes with chips. Joe even got to choose what filling he wanted in his omelette. He chose everything – tomatoes, mushrooms, bacon and lots of gooey melted cheese. He was right in the middle of a jaw-stretching mouthful when…

"It's about time we sorted out the bedrooms, Ron," said Mum to Dad. "Alex is too big for the cot. He's trying to climb out of it at night. His bed's got to go in Joe's room. Joe, you'd better stay in this afternoon to help move your stuff."

Joe choked on his mouthful of omelette. As he coughed, a bit of mushroom shot out towards Em.

"JOE!" she yelled. Joe hardly heard her.

"Move my stuff! Where? WHY?" he spluttered.

"Joe, what's this all about? You must have realised Alex couldn't carry on sleeping in our room. He's too big for the cot and your room is the only one big enough for another bed," said Mum. "If you stay here you can help me. Then I can arrange it as you like it."

"I don't like it! I don't want it arranged at all! I don't want Alex in my room! He's a baby and he cries in the night. It's MY room!" cried Joe.

"I'm sorry you hadn't understood what would happen, but we'll have to do it. There's no choice, Joe," said Dad. "Alex might hurt himself falling out of his cot."

Joe pushed his plate away. He didn't want the omelette any more.

"Joe, please eat that!" sighed Mum.

"I cooked it specially for you."

Joe forced some more mouthfuls down. As soon as he'd finished he jumped up and ran upstairs as fast as he could. He slammed his bedroom door and flung himself down on the bed. He grabbed his battered old ted and buried his face in his fur.

"I hate Mum!" he gulped. "I hate Dad! I hate Alex! Why don't they LEAVE ME ALONE!"

After a while he heard someone come in. Joe peered over the top of Ted's head. There was Mum.

"Joe, I'm really sorry," she said. "I guess it is hard to have a baby move into your room. Dad and I were talking about it. We wondered if you'd like the little bedroom, then Rob and Alex could share this one."

"Oh," said Joe. He thought about it. Then his eye fell on the computer. He liked playing computer games early in the morning.

"Can I have the computer in there?" he asked.

"Oh no!" said Mum, surprised. "It's such a small room. It'll be hard to fit everything in anyway. Those big boxes will have to go in the cupboard on the landing." She pointed at Joe's big box of Lego.

"I'll stay here, then," said Joe. "But it's not fair! This is my room and I like it like this!"

He jumped up and stumped crossly down the stairs, out of the house and off up the road. He was glad to get to his partly-built den. Fiercely, he began to pull the branches together.

"This is all I have now," he said out loud. "So it's going to be good. It's going to be the best den I've ever built."

Joe didn't stop working all afternoon. He collected branches and broke them to size. He pulled them into place and wove them in and out of each other. By the time it began to get dark the walls of the den were a lot higher. He had tree-bark stains all over his hands and clothes. He had bits of twig in his hair and a tear in his T-shirt. But he didn't care.

He stopped to stretch. When he stood up in his den, the walls reached his shoulders. He felt a little bit better. He wished he had a really good friend like Sam to show his den to. Then he set off back to the house where there was no room for him.

Chapter 2

Joe didn't like Sundays as much as Saturdays. He had to go to church without Sam. He really missed him. It also meant he couldn't watch the kids' programmes on TV for long. He was lounging in an armchair in his pyjamas watching his favourite show. He was munching a large bowl of cereal. There was at least another half hour before he had to move.

Mum didn't think so, though.

"Turn the TV off now please, Joe. Go and find your clothes."

"Oh, no, Mum! Only another five minutes!"

"Yes, and then another five minutes, and then another. I know you!" Mum took the controller. Joe's programme fizzled to a tiny dot and vanished.

"Put on clean jeans and your new jumper and WASH PROPERLY!" Mum's voice came floating up the stairs as Joe stumped off.

Blow church! thought Joe.

Later, sitting next to Mum in church, Joe was still thinking, Blow church! He'd missed his programmes and he was desperate to get out and finish his den.

It wasn't that he hated church, really. The band wasn't bad. The man who played acoustic guitar was great. They needed a new drummer though. The old one had moved away to another town. Sometimes they sang some good songs. Mum said perhaps he could have drum lessons soon. Joe pictured himself up there, playing a red and silver drum kit...

"Wake up, Joe," said Dad. "It's time for

Kids' Club."

Joe liked the games in Kids' Club but he didn't like sitting still. He'd heard the story before, too. It was Daniel in the lions' den. This guy, Daniel, was thrown into a lions' den because he prayed to God. How likely was that? Then God stopped the lions from eating him! What hungry lion would turn down a free meal?

"Let's act it out," said Katie, the Kids' Club leader. "Who'd like to be a lion?"

Wow! thought Joe, and put up his hand. So did most of the other boys.

"Now, who will be Daniel?" asked Katie. "What about you, Tom?"

Joe didn't like Tom very much. He always knew all the answers and he talked too much. Tom didn't like Joe very much, either.

Good! thought Joe, snarling and clawing in Tom's direction.

"Wait a minute, Joe," said Katie. "We haven't even sent Daniel to the lions' den yet!"

"Just practising!" said Joe with a growl.

Tom looked nervous.

But even when they did get to act it out, not much happened. The 'lions' weren't allowed to eat Tom, because they didn't in the story.

Baby stuff, thought Joe, scowling at Tom. He smirked back.

"How do you think Daniel felt when he was put in the den with those fierce lions?" asked Katie.

"Frightened," said Jade, a girl in the group.

"Yes," said Katie. "Those lions hadn't been fed. They would have been starving!"

Joe couldn't stand it any longer.

"Then why didn't they eat him?" he burst out.

"Because Daniel prayed to God and God stopped them. God looked after Daniel," said Katie. She looked at Joe. He scowled.

"You look puzzled, Joe."

"It's stupid. Lions are too fierce," said Joe.

"God's very strong," said Katie. "Do you ever get frightened of anything, Joe?"

Joe looked at his feet.

"Not much," he muttered.

"Well, if you ever are, try asking God to help you," said Katie. She gave out some activity sheets with puzzles on. Joe was glad she'd stopped looking at him.

They were getting ready to go home when there was a tap on Joe's shoulder. He looked up. It was the man from the allotments! Joe's heart sank. He looked at Dad's back ahead of him.

"It's all right!" said the man, laughing. "I just wanted to say hello. What's your name?"

Joe told him.

"Well, I'm Andy," said the man. "I wanted to tell you that I've used all the planks I need. There are some left – shorter ones. If you come to my allotment this afternoon I'll give them to you if you still want them."

Joe could hardly believe his ears.

"Oh, yes!" he said. "Thank you!"

"That's all right," said Andy. "My grandsons like making dens too."

Joe was very glad he'd come to church now.

But that afternoon Mum wanted Joe to clean his bedroom. Joe worked like fury. Even so, by the time he'd finished, it was nearly four o'clock. What if Andy had gone home? Joe went through the door so fast he nearly took off.

"Tea at five!" followed him out the door.

Joe crashed through the trees and ground to a halt at the fence behind the allotment hedge. Phew! There was Andy putting some plants in. A little boy was helping him. Andy waved at Joe.

"Come round to the gate. I'll meet you there," he said.

Joe screeched off along the road and round the corner to the big gate. There came his new friend with an armful of planks. The little boy was carrying some more.

"This is my grandson, Billy," said Andy. "He's visiting me today. I hope these are alright!" He held out the planks.

"Wow! Just what I need!" Joe said. "Thanks! Thanks, Billy."

Billy looked shy and grabbed Andy's hand.

"Can you manage?" said Andy, looking at him doubtfully as a plank slid off the pile. "I can help you carry them."

"Oh no!" said Joe. "You're busy and… and I don't want to waste your time."

"Oh, I'll be here till late tonight," said Andy. "I want to do some potting on of my spring cabbages. Ten minutes helping you won't make any difference."

"Oh no! Honest, I'll be fine, I really will!"
said Joe. Somehow he balanced the plank
on the others and staggered off as quickly as
he could. The thought of a grown up, even
one as helpful as Andy was turning out to
be, seeing his den, was awful. No one was
going to know!

Joe had a good time deciding where to put
the planks. He could get rid of those sticky-
out branches and use them all for the roof.
Or if he kept the branches and just used
some of the planks for the roof, he could
use some to sit on.

He was still making up his mind when he heard a voice in the distance. It was Em, calling him.

"Joe, come out! I know you're down here somewhere! It's past five and Mum's getting cross. Joe! JOE!"

Oh, no, thought Joe. She mustn't know where I've come from!

Quick as lightning Joe slithered out of the den. It had been a good move to make the

entrance at the back. He turned away from home and wriggled along the gap between the hedge and the allotment fence. Bits of branches snagged his clothes and a twig scratched his face. He must be making an awful noise with all this scrabbling along.

He paused for a moment to listen. Em was still there, sounding more annoyed.

"JOE! JO-OE! I'm going back! You'll be in trouble!"

Joe heard her footsteps fading up the road.

Wow! That was close, he thought. He made a mental note of the need to clear a good escape route in case this happened again. After all, foxes had two or three routes in and out of their dens for escaping. He waited a few minutes to let Em get home, and then wriggled out. No one was in sight. Joe hotfooted it for home.

Joe was lucky. When he got in, Mum was feeding Alex. He was up to his eyes in dinner and Mum was nearly as bad. She looked at Joe hard, but she couldn't do anything or even say much. Alex kept grabbing the spoon, handfuls of dinner and poor Mum's hair as fast as he could. Joe sank thankfully into his chair and started eating.

Chapter 3

Joe groaned when he looked out of the window in the morning. Rain was sheeting down. It looked nearly as dark as night. Glumly, he went downstairs. Mum was rushing about looking for wellies and raincoats.

It was another two days before the sun came out again. Joe couldn't bear it. He had no one to play with. Each day he tried to go out to his den but there were such deep, muddy puddles on the path he slipped over and got all covered in mud. Mum wasn't very happy with him when he came home.

"As if I haven't got enough cleaning up to do with Alex and Rob!" she sighed. "I know, Joe. Go and get changed and then you can help me make a cake."

Joe enjoyed that. But when it was finished he had nothing to do again. Em was watching a boring chat show on the television. He couldn't go upstairs because Alex was having a nap in *his* bedroom. Rob had set up a Lego war zone over most of the kitchen floor. Joe had to lie down on the hall floor to draw a den plan.

Dad tripped over him when he came in. He looked at Joe.

"All getting on top of you, is it, Joe?" he asked. "Never mind. Listen to that wind. It'll soon dry things up!"

Yes! thought Joe. Perhaps I'll be able to do some more repair work after school tomorrow.

"Bye, Joe!" called Mum as Joe tugged his school backpack through the front door next morning. "Have a good day at school.

Got your lunch money and PE kit – oh, and your reading book?"

"Oh, bother, reading book," said Joe. He never forgot his PE kit. Somehow he didn't think his reading book was so important. His teacher, Mrs Harper, didn't agree. Joe started looking. He couldn't find it anywhere.

"Oh, no!" wailed Joe. He started frantically throwing things about.

"What's the matter?" asked Rob, chewing his toothbrush in the doorway.

"I can't find my reading book!" said Joe. He looked at Rob. "I don't suppose you've seen it, have you?"

"Has it got an aeroplane on the front?" bubbled Rob through the toothpaste.

"Er... yes, I think so," said Joe. He remembered how much Rob liked planes.

"It's here," said Rob. He brought it out of his own room.

"Oh, thanks," breathed Joe. He grabbed the book and leapt down the stairs.

"Bring it again," called Rob after him. "I like the pictures."

Joe pulled a face. The speed he got through reading books, it'd be coming home for another two weeks! Then he thought of his den and smiled. Never mind. That den was going to be the best one he'd ever made!

Joe went slowly through the school gates and wandered over to his classroom door. The playground seemed strangely empty.

I must be very early for school, he thought.

Joe used to walk to school with Sam and talk to him while they waited for the bell to ring. Now it often seemed no one wanted to play with him. There were usually some boys chatting or kicking a ball about, though. Sometimes Joe could join in with that. But there was no one there today.

Then he spotted a group of boys close together in another corner. Joe wondered what was going on. A boy called Mike saw him and ran over.

"Come over here, Joe. Lee says he's got a new knife!"

"Has he brought it to school?" asked Joe excitedly. It was against school rules to bring knives or even toy guns to school.

They joined the group of boys clustered in the farthest corner of the playground.

"Hi, Lee, have you really got a new knife?" asked Joe.

"What's it to you, titch?" asked Lee's friend, Nick. "Mind your own business." He took a step towards Joe. Joe moved back. Nick was a bully. He'd hurt a boy Joe knew.

"Hold on, Nick, it's okay," said Lee. He was enjoying showing off about his knife.

"Dad bought it for me," he said to Joe. "It's really for scuba diving. He says I can learn when I'm bigger. It's about this long." He made a wide gap with his hands. "It's very strong. It's got a great sheath. It's black."

Lee was older than Joe. He'd be changing schools next year. He always had something new. He had a fantastic bike and some great designer clothes that he even

wore to school. The head teacher didn't like it but Lee's parents didn't care. Joe and Mike and most other people had to wear school uniform.

That day Joe couldn't stop thinking about Lee's knife. It could really help him to make his den! If it was very strong, he could use it to cut those branches right down to size. Then he found himself behind Lee in the dinner queue.

"Hey, Lee. I'd really like to see your knife. Do you think you could show it to me after school?"

Lee looked at Joe.

"I was going down the shop for some

sweets," he said. "What's in it for me?"

Joe panicked. He'd got to get his hands on that knife.

"I-I'll show you my den!" he blurted. "My gran gave me some sweets – a big bag! We could eat them!"

"Okay," said Lee. "Don't forget them. I'll go home to get my knife and I'll meet you at the park gate."

It was a wonderful knife – shiny and deadly looking.

"You use it like this to lever shellfish off rocks underwater," said Lee, showing Joe on some bracken and a tree seedling nearby. "It'll slice through any seaweed and stuff you want to collect and bring up with you. It'd even cut through this." He laid a small branch on the ground and cut the end off.

"Do this one, too," said Joe. Together they trimmed some of the branches Joe had found yesterday.

"This den isn't bad," said Lee grudgingly. "No one can see you and it only needs a bit more work to cut the branches for the roof. I've got to go now, though."

"Do you think I could borrow the knife?" asked Joe eagerly. "It'd take me half the time to finish the den."

"We-ell... okay," said Lee. "But only till Wednesday." He grabbed Joe's arm. "You look after it. I won't be pleased if anything happens to it and neither will Big Nick and Darren." He named his two friends at school. Everyone was careful around them.

Joe quaked.

"I-I'll look after it, I promise," he said.

After Lee went, Joe worked till tea-time. The branches lay much closer together with all the bits trimmed off. He filled in the roof and stuffed bracken in the cracks. It wouldn't completely keep out the rain, but it looked much better, like a small dark cave.

Joe didn't dare take the knife home. Mum would have a fit if she saw it. Joe put it carefully in its sheath and wrapped it in a plastic bag. Then he hid it beneath the roots of an old tree at the side of his den and covered it with dead leaves. It should be safe there!

Chapter 4

Next morning, Joe was first downstairs.

"Hello, Joe! Are you all right?" asked Mum. She watched in amazement as Joe galloped past her towards the cereal cupboard. Joe wasn't famous for getting up this early.

"Yes, I'm fine. I've got something to do. I want to go early," gabbled Joe as the milk splashed on to his cereal.

"Is it football practice this morning?" Mum asked. Joe spluttered into his cereal.

"When is your next football game?" she went on. "Rob and I want to come and cheer you on."

Joe swallowed his mouthful and thought hard. He liked Mum to come and cheer for him, but right now he was desperate to get out of the door.

"I think it's the Saturday after next," he said, and took another big spoonful.

"Well, find out and let me know," said Mum, "and can you... oh dear." There was a wail from Alex upstairs. Mum went out of the room in a hurry.

"Make sure you're not late for school," she said as she went.

"Yes, Mum," said Joe, between mouthfuls. He put down his bowl, grabbed his backpack and escaped before she decided to stop him.

It was a lot dryer today, but Joe's cheeks were cold. Twigs cracked under his feet as he pushed through the trees. He had to climb over a bough that had fallen over the path. He stumbled over some more branches. He stood rigid. Something was wrong. Those branches weren't there yesterday. He peered ahead. There was a lot of broken stuff around. Was his den all right? Anxiously, he pushed forward.

"Oh no!" he burst out. There *was* no den! There was a hollow in the ground with broken branches, dead leaves and bits of planking scattered about. Joe picked up a bit of plank with numb fingers.

"Who did it?" he wailed. No one knew about his den. But wait... His mind went back to last night. Lee! Lee knew. But Lee had liked his den. He had even lent him his knife... the knife! Where was the knife?

Frantically Joe scrabbled among the

broken branches. He yanked them out of the way, desperate to get to the tree roots where he had hidden the knife last night. It wasn't there! It must be! Joe hunted all around.

As he tore at the rubbish that was his den, Joe's breath came in gasps. What would those boys do to him? Last year they had beaten a boy up. He'd had bruises for two weeks! Joe sank down on to a pile of sticks. What could he do?

As Joe sat there hopelessly, he caught sight of his watch. Eight fifty! He'd got five minutes to get all the way to school! He jumped up and charged up the road, his bag banging on his back. Could he make it? The school bell began to ring. Joe tore along the road and into the playground. He skidded to the end of his class's line just as it vanished inside the building.

Joe couldn't stop his gasps for breath. Mrs Harper, his teacher, looked up.

"What have you been doing to get in such a state, Joe?" she asked. "You're filthy and you've got leaves in your hair. Go and clean yourself up. You can't work like that!"

"Sorry," said Joe. He went out to the washbasins.

"Where have you been, Joe?" asked Mrs Harper when he came back in.

"I-I was messing about in the wood," said Joe. "I forgot the time."

"Oh. From now on, try to remember it, please!"

But things went from bad to worse. Joe couldn't remember anything. He answered questions wrong. He couldn't finish his work on time. He was scared stiff he'd meet Lee. At lunch-time he was looking out for Lee all the time and keeping out of his way.

"What's wrong, Joe?" asked Mike. But Joe didn't want to tell Mike. Mike was all right, but Joe hadn't known him that long. He didn't want it to get back to Lee that he'd lost the knife. Lee wanted it back tomorrow, so he still had tonight to find it.

After school Joe hunted again. He searched carefully this time, moving all the broken

stuff away from the den, sorting through it
and looking under it as he went. He was
working so hard he wasn't aware of
anything else.

"Found you!" said a voice. Joe whirled
round. There, leaning on a tree with her
arms folded was Em.

"What are you doing, spying on me?"
cried Joe.

"Mum wants you. It's late. Anyway, what
are you doing with all this mess?" said Em.

"It's not mess – or at least it wasn't!" said

Joe, hotly. "It was a den. It was a good one, too." It didn't matter if Em knew now. It was ruined anyway.

"Who wrecked it?" asked Em.

"I'm not sure," said Joe, "but I think it was Lee Granger." Suddenly it all seemed too much. He looked at Em. She wasn't laughing. "I've lost his knife too."

Joe told Em all about it.

"Wow, Joe!" said Em when he'd finished. "Lee Granger's tough."

"I know," said Joe. They sat silently.

"Tell you what, though," said Em, "if it was Lee, he'll have taken his own knife back."

"Of course," said Joe. He was quiet. "But if it wasn't?"

"Maybe we can find out," said Em. "Let's look around. There might be some clues."

They hunted around a bit.

"Hey, Joe," called Em, "look over here."

At the back of the den, where Joe's escape route used to be, the tree branches were all broken down.

"They went out this way," said Em. "Let's see if we can find out where they went."

Joe looked at Em in amazement. She wasn't as thick as he'd thought!

Together they pushed through. Sure enough, the ground was trampled and the branches of the bushes were broken back where someone had crashed through. With his heart beating fast, Joe set off along the trail, Em close behind.

After a little while the trail moved away from the allotments where the copse broadened out. There was a group of holly trees ahead. Joe and Em peered through to the gap in the middle of them. There, in the middle, was a heap of planks and branches. Joe looked round. There was nobody in sight.

"Come on," he said.

They bent low and carefully made their way through the prickly branches.

"This is stuff from my den," said Joe sadly. There were some of Andy's planks. "What are they going to do with all this wood?"

"It's a bonfire," said Em. "I expect they didn't have time to light it last night."

They looked at each other.

"Do you think they'll be coming back tonight?" said Joe.

"They might," said Em.

"D'you think we could come back and see?" said Joe.

"Why not?" said Em, her eyes glinting.

"Mum won't let us out when it's dark," said Joe.

"She'll let me out if I say I need to see Sarah about my homework," said Em.

"You go to bed – you have to go earlier than me anyway. I can sneak round and put the ladder under your window. You can come down and hide somewhere. Then I'll go back in after a bit, pretend I've been to Sarah's and go to bed. I can easily get out of my window, 'cos my room's downstairs. I've done it before."

"Wow!" said Joe. "We can hump up our bedclothes in case Mum looks in."

"What if we're caught?" said Em.

"Oh, early beds for a week," said Joe, carelessly. He thought to himself that there might actually be more trouble than that.

"Mmm," said Em.

"Oh, who cares?" Joe shrugged. "I've got to know who wrecked my den."

"We need to know where that knife is, too," said Em.

They set off for home. Joe felt better now there was something he could do. He looked at Em. Who'd have thought she would join in something like this? Perhaps sisters weren't so bad after all!

Chapter 5

The meal seemed to go on for ever. Alex threw his spoon in Dad's dinner. Dinner went all over the table and all over Dad. Joe and Rob both thought it was very funny, but Dad didn't. They had to wait while all the mess was cleaned up. Then Mum wanted to know about a birthday disco Em had been invited to. She was worried in case there weren't going to be any grown-ups there.

"I think Sarah's mum will be there," said Em.

"Do you *know* she will?" asked Mum.

"No, but I'll ask," said Em. Then Mum

wanted to know how late it went on. Nothing Em said seemed to stop Mum worrying. In the end Alex started crying. Mum dumped the pudding in front of them and took him out. Em and Joe ate it as fast as they could.

Alex cried a lot that evening. Mum thought he might be teething. Joe felt sorry it was hurting Alex so much, but it meant Mum was too busy looking after him to take much notice of them. Dad was on a night shift so he had to get ready for work.

"Go and get ready for bed," whispered Em. "No one will notice it's a bit early."

Joe wrapped his big dressing gown over his clothes when he went to say goodnight to Mum. He looked a bit fat. Mum was walking up and down with Alex in her arms. She was pleased to see him all ready.

"Joe, I'm really pleased you're being so helpful," she said. "Do you think you could run the bath water and get Rob into the bath for me?"

Oh no! Joe thought to himself. He filled

the bath as quickly as he could.

"Don't want to!" said Rob.

"Oh, come on!" begged Joe. How could he get Rob to hurry up? He'd got to be ready for Em! Then he had a brainwave.

"You can borrow my rocket model to play with in the bath," he said.

"Wow!" said Rob. "Thanks!"

"How kind, Joe!" said Mum. "You're being such a help to me!"

Joe felt a bit bad, but not bad enough to bother him very much. He climbed into bed and sat up, listening. After a while he heard a clunk under his window. He opened it and leaned out. There was the ladder and there was Em at the bottom, holding it firm.

"Hurry up!" she hissed. "Dad will need to get his bike from the shed to go to work."

Joe's heart gave a lurch. They hadn't thought of that! Dad used his bike for night shifts. He bundled some clothes in a lump under his bedclothes. He climbed on to the windowsill and lay on his front with his legs poking out. Carefully he put a foot on the

top rung of the ladder. It only just reached!
Slowly he moved backwards till he was
safely on it.

At the bottom he helped Em lower the
ladder down. Then they heard whistling. It
was Dad coming round the side of the
house.

"Put it down!" whispered Joe. They
dropped the ladder. Together they leaped
behind the shrubs in the flowerbed.

Dad went whistling up the path to the
shed. Joe's heart was thumping so loud he
thought Dad must be able to hear it! But

Dad was thinking about something else. He didn't notice the ladder lying in the dark near the flowerbed. He got out his bike, locked the shed and cheerfully pedalled off. Joe and Em heard his whistling dying away down the road.

"Wow! That was a close shave. Where are you going to wait?" said Em.

"Round the back of the shed," said Joe. "There are some bricks I can sit on."

"I'll be as quick as I can," said Em. She ran off.

Joe went behind the shed. Yes, he was out of sight here. He piled the old bricks together and sat down in the dark. He scrunched up with his arms round his knees. He tried to think what Em was doing.

Surely by now she was in the bathroom. He gave her time to pretend to do her teeth and get washed. Mum had to hear bathroom noises. Then Em had to get warm clothes on, hump up the bed and climb out of the window. She would be coming... now. But she didn't come. Joe decided to count to one hundred. Just as he got to fifty-six there was a rustle behind him. Joe jumped up and spun round, his hair on end.

"It's only me! Be quiet or we'll have Mum out," whispered Em. She was trying not to giggle.

"You pig!" hissed Joe.

"Oh, it was only a joke!" said Em. "Anyway, it's all working okay. Alex keeps going to sleep then waking up again crying. Mum will never miss us."

Together they crept down the garden path and down the side of the house. They peered round the front of the house. The lounge curtains were drawn, so no one would notice them. Joe tiptoed out and down the path. Then they heard the phone ring.

"Quick, Em, come on!" whispered Joe frantically. The phone was by the front door under a little window. Mum would be able to see them if she looked out. They both bent low and scurried down to the gate. Just as Em latched it behind her, Mum picked up the phone.

"Good for Alex!" muttered Em. Alex was still crying and Mum was jigging him up and down in one arm with the phone in her other hand. Em grinned at Joe. They bobbed down below the level of the hedge and ran down the road.

Chapter 6

Once they were out of sight of the house, they stood up.

"We've been ages already," said Em.

"Come on, quick!" said Joe.

They hurried through the trees. It was different at night. There were noises and rustles Joe never heard during the day. He jumped as something scuttled away near his foot. He was glad Em was there.

They were making plenty of rustles themselves. Em tripped over a root.

"Be quiet!" hissed Joe. Then crack, a twig broke under his foot.

"You be quiet!" said Em. "I hurt my leg!"

"Ssh! Look!" whispered Joe. He could see a wavering light through the trees ahead. The bonfire must be alight! They stood still for a minute.

"Come on," said Em. They picked their way carefully through the trees. Joe heard faint voices and laughter. The light became brighter and the branches of trees around and over the fire showed up here and there as flames darted out. The voices got louder. Em grabbed Joe's arm.

"Don't get too close. They'll see us!" she whispered.

Joe crouched down behind a clump of holly. He peered round it. Em came close beside him. There they were, four big boys, their shapes black against the fire.

A voice Joe knew rang out.

"That Joe will be shaking in his bed tonight!" It was Lee.

"Yep! He knows what'll be waiting for him tomorrow when he turns up without this!" That was Nick's sneering laughter, and he was waving something about that glinted in the firelight. Joe's insides were churning. He looked at Em.

"That's the knife," he whispered. "There's nothing we can do."

"Just listen a bit," whispered Em. "They're pigs. They ruined your den. We're not giving up yet."

Anger rose in Joe. Em was right.

"Give me that!" said an older boy. Joe didn't know him. Someone passed him a giant chocolate bar and he broke off a chunk.

"Great!" said Lee. "Where did you get that? Let's have some." The chocolate was shared out. It was the size Joe only ever got on his birthdays. Nick put the knife down to eat. Joe couldn't take his eyes off it. He began to move forward. If he could just reach it... then he felt Em grab his ankle.

"No!" she hissed. Joe pulled away.

"I can do it so they won't see me," he whispered back. He pulled harder and wriggled.

"What's that? I heard a noise!" one of the boys said. Joe froze. Em let go of his ankle.

"Nah, it's nothing," someone replied. "You're just scared because you nicked your dad's chocolate!"

There was a laugh. More chunks were broken off. Joe breathed a sigh of relief. He wriggled closer. They seemed to have forgotten about the knife. He could nearly reach it, he was sure. He waited for his chance. Next time there was a gale of laughter he reached out. Ever so slowly...he had it! He moved carefully back towards Em. She watched with amazement.

"Wow! That's great!"

"Come on! Let's try and get away," whispered Joe.

Holding their breath the two moved quietly, step by step. Then, just as they drew close to the nearest trees, a cry rang out.

"The knife! My knife's gone!"

Suddenly all of the gang were shouting, looking.

"Quick, behind the trees!" whispered Em. But it was too late.

"There's someone there!" shouted Lee.

"Run!" said Joe.

Joe and Em leapt away. But, although they knew the wood, everything was different in the dark. Joe ran, his breath coming in gasps, dodging trees, jumping over brambles, the branches lashing his face. Behind, he could hear crashing and swearing. All of a sudden there was nothing under his racing feet. He crashed down. Before he could get up, a hand grabbed his coat.

"Got you, you little thief! You're coming with me." Joe's arms were pulled behind him and he was pushed and shoved through the trees.

In between his gasps for breath he heard Em cry out.

"Have you got the other one, Matt?" called the boy who held him.

"Yes. It's a girl!"

Joe and Em were pulled into the firelight. Em was limping.

"It's him! Little sneak!" yelled Lee.

"You're the sneak! Breaking my den! Making me think I'd lost your knife!" Joe was so mad he couldn't see.

"No, Joe!" He heard Em's frightened voice. Then, OOOOF! His legs were knocked from under him. His face slammed into the leaves as he fell to the ground.

"That'll teach you!" Someone grabbed him and dragged him up. It was Big Nick.

His fist was clenched.

"Stop it, Nick. He's just a kid," said one of boys.

Nick snarled. He gave Joe a great shove. Joe fell with a smash against a nearby tree. He couldn't get up. There was a silence. Then he heard Em sobbing.

"He's bleeding," he heard someone say. "Nick, you idiot! What've you done?"

"Aw, he's all right," growled Nick.

Someone grabbed Joe roughly and turned him over. There were some gasps.

"Oh no! You've done it this time, Nick!"

"Look at his face!"

"I'm getting out of here!"

There was a scramble as the boys turned and ran off towards the road, smashing through the branches and swearing as they stumbled over roots. On the edge of the firelight, Nick suddenly turned round.

"You watch what you say," he hissed at Joe and Em. "Lee's my friend, remember."

He ran back and waved the knife close to Joe's face before turning and following the others as they crashed off through the woods. Joe quaked, still lying on his side with the sticky blood trickling into his eye. Thankfully he heard the crashes and thumps fade off into the distance.

Chapter 7

The wood was quiet. Even the fire had stopped crackling. There was just the odd flame deep inside and cracks of red in the embers round the edge.

Joe swallowed painfully. His nose hurt so much where it had slammed into the tree that he wondered if it was broken. He managed to twist his head slowly towards Em. Her face was smudged and dirty. It looked white in the faint light coming from the dying fire. Her hair was straggling across her face.

"What are we going to do?" croaked Joe.

Em looked at Joe.

"I don't know," she whispered. "Your

face is a mess," she said. "Does it hurt a
lot?"

Joe slowly turned on his side and pushed
himself up. He gasped and put his hands
round his nose. It throbbed. He sat very
still. It was better like that.

Joe was cold. The night noises seemed
louder. After a minute Em struggled up.

"Perhaps we can get the fire going again,"
she said.

She took a stick and set off towards the
fire, but when she tried to put her foot down
she cried out and fell down on her knees.

"I can't walk!" she groaned.

"We could yell for help," said Joe.

"There's no one near," said Em. "The houses don't start before our road."

"But we don't want to stay here all night," Joe shivered. "If you can't walk I suppose I'll have to go for help." He didn't feel very sure about it, though. His nose and head hurt so much he couldn't remember which way they'd come from.

"But how will you find the way in the dark?" Em's voice was wobbly.

"There is one thing we can do," said Joe, slowly. "We had a story at Kids' Club about Daniel. Katie said if we're frightened we could pray." He was quiet for a moment. "Would it do any good?"

"Well, it can't do any harm," said Em, sounding a bit braver.

That was true, thought Joe. If God really did help Daniel, maybe he would help them.

"I'm going to, anyway," said Em. She shut her eyes.

"God, will you please help us?" she said quietly.

Joe waited. Nothing happened. He waited some more.

All of a sudden he felt really mad. Why should those boys get away with it? He stood up. His nose was really hurting but he didn't care. He went to the edge of the clearing. If only he could remember which way the road was. Then, as if someone had heard his thought, he heard the faint sound of a car in the distance.

He turned round.

"Hey, Em, the road's over there. I heard a car. That means the allotments are the other way. All I've got to do is go that way till I find the fence and follow it round! Then I know where I am and I can get home!"

"But it'll take you ages," said Em. "Look, try and help me! Perhaps I can manage to walk if you help me."

Joe took Em's arm. She hopped a few steps, but her poor foot was dangling behind and it hurt a lot. Then she leaned too much on Joe and they both fell over.

"It's no good," panted Joe. "It'll take too

long. Come back to the fire."

They struggled back and sat in an unhappy silence.

Joe suddenly had an idea.

"Andy gave me some planks. He's got an allotment here. He sometimes works there late. It's a lot nearer. He's nice. If he's there he'd help us!"

"See if you can get the fire going again

first. It'd make me feel better," said Em. "You need little bits of stuff like dead leaves. Here." She held some out.

Joe took the handful of dead leaves and prodded the middle of the heap of ashes with a big stick. It was still red inside! He carefully put the leaves on the reddest place. Nothing happened.

"You need to blow," said Em.

Joe leaned towards the fire as far as he could. It hurt his nose a lot, but he tried to blow a bit. It made him feel dizzy.

"This isn't working," he said and sat back down again. "I need to go soon. What if Andy goes home? If he's there. It's getting late."

"Here," said Em urgently, "waft it with this!" She held out a bit of plank to Joe.

Joe grabbed it and flapped hard at the glow. The red got a bit brighter. He flapped harder. The dead leaves glowed red at the edges and crinkled.

"Some more leaves!" cried Joe.

"Here!" panted Em. She was scrabbling

around where she could reach. "We need some small twigs, too!"

Joe shoved the leaves on and wafted them some more.

"Please, God, please!" he muttered. A little flame shot out for a second. Em handed him some little twigs. They caught light quicker this time. There were some bits of wood near the edge of the fire that hadn't burned up. When the twigs were burning Joe put the bits of wood carefully across the glowing leaves. He sat back and held his breath.

"Yes!" he yelled as they began to burn.

"Can you collect some more?" asked Em. "I'll need to feed it while you're gone."

"I must go and look for Andy soon!" said Joe. He went round the clearing as fast as he could. He managed to collect some twigs and one or two bigger branches. Then he helped Em get nearer to the fire so she could reach to put wood on. Looking at the fire, Joe felt a lot better. The cold, miserable feeling in his stomach seemed to be vanishing as it crackled away. Even his nose seemed to hurt less.

"I'll be all right now," said Em. "You go now. We can't stay here all night. But hurry!"

"I'll be as quick as I can," promised Joe.

Chapter 8

Joe set off. The darkness grew thicker as he left the glow of the fire behind. He went as fast as he could, but every time he banged into something his head hurt. The wood had so many stones and stumps, sticky-out branches and roots in it. Somehow he managed to stumble along. Now he didn't have Em to talk to he could hear all sorts of other noises, rustles of things moving... and squeaks and moans.

What were those moans? Ghosts? His breath came fast. Then there was a breath of wind and a creak nearby. Joe froze. Then he felt a gust of wind. WIND! It was blowing the branches and making them rub together! When he'd been building his den he'd noticed branches made that squeaky, groaning noise as they rubbed together. Joe breathed again and went on.

"OW!" he yelled. Some prickly branches swept across his arm. A holly bush! He hadn't seen it in the dark. He rubbed his arm. There was a big scratch. It felt wet. So now his arm was bleeding as well. Joe sat down. How was he ever going to get to the allotments? He thought of poor Em, stuck

by the fire on her own, waiting. He had to go on. Painfully he set off again.

This time he kept feeling ahead so as not to bang into anything else. He seemed to be getting on better when he felt the ground go down. He sat down and felt around with his feet. Where was he? He stretched his foot down. Water!

"It's the ditch!" he said in relief. The ditch ran all round the allotments on two sides. Joe knew that the allotment fence was on the other side of the ditch, though he couldn't see it. He still had to cross the ditch and move along the fence quite a way before he reached the gate. What if Andy wasn't there?

"Shut up!" he told himself fiercely. "Go and see!"

Carefully, he lowered himself down. His feet went in the water. It was very squelchy.

"Yuk!" said Joe out loud. But he had no choice. The ditch was too wide to jump across with his head feeling like this. His legs went lower and lower. It was very muddy, but when the water got just over his knees, his legs stopped going down. Joe pushed off from the bank and tipped himself over the ditch. Then he lay on his stomach on the other bank and pulled. His leg wouldn't come out! He was stuck in the mud!

"Oh no!" he puffed. It had to come out. He pulled again. No good! What could he do? He rested his head on his hands for a minute. As he looked up he caught a glimpse of... could it be? Yes, it was... light! It was just a crack around a door, but it was light! Someone was there. Perhaps it was Andy. He didn't have to crawl round to the gate! He could yell! Andy might hear him!

"HELP! HELP! HELP! HELP!" Joe went on yelling and yelling.

Joe was running out of breath. Then, just as he opened his mouth for a final shout, there was a crack of branches breaking. Someone smashed through the trees on the other side of the fence, a torch beam waving madly as he ran.

"What's this? What's the matter? Goodness me!" said a man's voice all in one breath. He shone the beam through the fence at Joe.

"I know you! It's the boy with the planks! Joe, isn't it? What on earth's happened?"

"Andy, please help us!" croaked Joe.

"Wait!" said Andy. Joe could see the torchlight bouncing along as Andy ran towards the gate. Before long there was a crashing noise as Andy forced his way through the trees to reach Joe.

Andy shone the torch in the ditch before he clambered down, splashed into the water and took hold of Joe round the waist. Joe's nose banged against Andy's chest.

"OW!" yelled Joe. "My nose is hurt, Andy!"

"Sorry!" said Andy. He bent down and gently freed Joe's legs. Before he knew it Joe was sitting safely on the bank.

"What's happened, Joe?" asked Andy. "No, wait, let's get you where it's warm first."

"No, Andy, Em!" said Joe. "We've got to go and get her! She's hurt her leg! She can't walk!"

"Who?" said Andy. "Who's Em? Where is she?"

"My sister," said Joe. He tried to tell Andy where Em was.

"Well, I can't leave you here," said Andy. "I'll take you to my shed and go back for Em. If there's light from this fire you're talking about, I'll find her."

Joe hung on to Andy as he carried him carefully through the wood. His head hurt so much now, but he was so glad he'd found Andy he didn't care. In the shed, Andy moved the trays and pots of little plants he'd been working on and arranged an old coat in a corner. He propped Joe up on it next to a bag of garden compost.

"I'll be back before you know it," said Andy. He shoved a packet of biscuits and a bottle of water at Joe and was gone.

Joe felt too sick for biscuits but he was very thirsty. He drank some water. His head was throbbing. He rested it on the bag of compost. It didn't seem long before the door opened again. Andy was back already, carrying Em.

Andy had a flask of hot chocolate. He wrapped Em in an old jumper and poured them all a drink. With a mug of chocolate in his hands, Joe felt a little better. They told Andy all about what had happened.

"Hmm," Andy said, "there's going to be some trouble from this night's work, I can see! It's a good thing I had all that potting on to do – and that you remembered, Joe. You could have been there all night!"

"I prayed," said Em.

"Then that's it!" said Andy. "There's

never a prayer prayed that God doesn't hear. God helped Joe get here. But I've got to get you both home quick, that's the long and short of it. Neither of you look very good."

Once more Andy picked Em up and the three of them made their way back through the wood. Andy put his other arm round Joe to help him along. Joe was in such a daze that when they got home he only heard Mum's voice faintly as she cried out when she saw them. He woke up a bit because it hurt when Mum washed him and he couldn't help screaming when she touched his nose.

"Poor Joe," said Mum. "We'd better take you to hospital. Em needs an X-ray and you might too."

Joe drifted in and out of sleep while he was carried around and his nose was prodded, X-rayed and washed. When he finally got home his bed had never felt so good.

Chapter 9

The next thing Joe knew, he was still in bed and the sunshine was hurting his eyes. His head ached. The door opened and Rob's head came round it.

"He's awake, Mum!" he yelled.

Mum appeared.

"Oh, good, you're awake," she said. "The doctor's here. Now, Rob, if you're staying in here, sit over there, out of the way."

The doctor looked at Joe's scratched arm and his swollen nose.

"You'll have to rest up a bit to give that chance to heal before you go out," he said. He looked at Joe's mum.

"I hope you're going to contact the police. Those boys must be stopped." He looked at Joe sternly. "Not that you haven't been a very silly boy yourself!"

"Yes, he has," said Mum. "His dad and I have a few things to say to him. The police are coming later."

Joe quaked. The police!

After she had seen the doctor out, Mum came back. This time she had a big tray of breakfast. Cereal, bacon, scrambled egg and beans! Joe's nose was sore whenever he opened his mouth, but somehow he managed to stretch it enough to get all that in. Mum and Alex stayed in the room while he ate it. He liked them being there.

Mum smiled when he had finished.

"If you can eat all that there's not much wrong," she said. She gave Joe a quick hug.

"Oh, Joe, you've frightened me to death! What did you do that for?"

"I'm really sorry, Mum," said Joe. His head hurt a lot.

Mum stroked his hair gently.

"Go to sleep for a bit," she said. "You're all right now."

It was a policewoman who came to see Joe. He had to tell her all about the four boys and about the knife. She was quite nice. At the end she shook her head.

"You have been very lucky," she said. "At least one of those boys has been in trouble before. You could have been badly hurt."

Joe thought about it. He wasn't so sure it was luck. He remembered Em's prayer. Perhaps God did have something to do with it.

Joe's mum and dad were there while Joe talked to the policewoman. After the policewoman left, Dad came in to Joe's room again.

"Joe, you've got to promise me there'll be no more messing about with knives or sneaking out at night," he said.

Joe remembered the knife flashing as Nick waved it round.

"Dad," he gasped, "they'll get me! That big boy said they would if I told!"

"I'm sure the police will take care of that!" Dad said grimly. "It's not being able to trust you that I don't like. It's very important to be able to trust people. You knew we wouldn't want you to use a sharp knife, and if you hadn't deceived Mum and sneaked out like that, this wouldn't have happened."

He looked at Joe. Joe felt his ears going hot.

"I think you'll have to stay in after school and at weekends until I can trust you again," said Dad.

"Oh, Dad!" gasped Joe. Stuck for ever in the house with Mum, Rob, Alex and Em... Em!

"Is Em all right?" he asked.

"Yes, apart from her sprained ankle. The policewoman talked to her too. As for her, she really should have known better!" Dad stood up.

"Dad, she was only trying to help me. She was great!" said Joe.

"I don't quite see it like that," said Dad. "But it's a good thing you're getting on better, because you'll be spending a lot of time in together from now on!"

Joe had to stay in bed for three days. The TV made his head ache. He didn't want to read. When he tried to move around his head hurt. When he ate his mouth and nose hurt. And even when he got better he wouldn't be allowed out! He was really fed up. He couldn't stand Rob around. He snapped at Alex. He grumbled at Mum. When she told him off, he even grumbled at God.

"God," he said, "I thought you got me out of that mess. If you really care, get me out of this one!"

When Em felt better she came to see him.

"You think yourself lucky!" she said. "Dad says I can't go away on the youth group weekend."

"Oh no!" said Joe. "I'm sorry. You were great, Em!"

Em looked a bit happier.

"Oh well," she said, "it was quite exciting. I can go back to school tomorrow, anyway."

The next day was even worse. Joe was so bored he wanted to scream. After lunch he tried to do a puzzle. Even that had a piece missing.

Then the doorbell rang. It was Andy!

"I came to see how you are," he said. "Your mum says you're driving her mad!"

"Everything's driving me mad!" said Joe.

"Well, I've got an idea," said Andy. "When you're better, you can come and help me with my allotment. I could do with the help. Then I would let you have a corner of my allotment to build a hut or den on. It would be all your own and no one would damage it because it's on my allotment."

Stars went off in Joe's head.

"Wow!" he said.

He sat up without thinking and hurt his head. But life suddenly seemed interesting again. Then his heart sank.

"I'm not allowed out!" He told Andy what Dad had said.

"Your dad might let you do it if I'm there," said Andy. "I'll go and talk to him."

"I'm not sure he deserves it," said Dad, "but I think he's been through a lot. Well, I'll tell you what. If you can behave yourself at home at weekends for a month, Joe, and if you really don't mind keeping an eye on him, Andy, he can come to the allotment then."

"YES!" shouted Joe. A proper clubhouse! His own place for ever!

Chapter 10

It was a very long month. One good thing about it was that Joe missed school for the first two weeks while his nose and head got better. He had plenty of time during the long days to draw lots of plans for his clubhouse and collect building materials. Dad saved bits of wood for him. When he was a bit better Mum let Joe go out with her to the shop. He bought some chocolate and cola to keep him going while he was building the clubhouse.

Andy bought a new spade for him. Joe wasn't quite so keen on that. He began to get a bit interested in the potatoes and runner beans Andy wanted to plant though, particularly when Andy said he could have some himself if he worked hard.

Joe had to miss church for those two weeks. He was very surprised when his Kids' Club leader, Katie, came to see him. They talked about TV programmes and videos. Katie told him about a good video about Daniel in the lions' den. She said she'd try and get it for Joe to watch.

"God helped me like he helped Daniel," said Joe. He gasped. That had popped out of his mouth before he'd had time to think!

"How?" asked Katie.

"Well, those big boys were like the lions and we were stuck there with them," said Joe.

Then he told Katie about Em's prayer.

"That's fantastic!" said Katie. "Now you really know God cares!"

"I guess he does," said Joe thoughtfully.

Another person who came to see Joe was his friend from school, Mike. Mike and Joe hadn't been friends long because Mike had only just started to come to Joe's school. Joe was a lot better, but he was very bored having to stay at home. He felt very glad to see Mike.

Mike spotted Em's crutches as he came in. Em had leaned them against the wall by the front door.

"Hey, they're cool crutches," said Mike. "Can I have a go?"

"They're just crutches," said Joe. "You can if you want."

Mike hopped round the room a bit.

"Watch me!" he said.

He leaned against the wall and set the crutches a long way in front of him. Then he took a great leap, leaning on the crutches. He went flying out and landed nearly all the way across the room. He staggered a bit, then grinned at Joe.

"Let me have a go!" said Joe.

He couldn't get quite as far as Mike. He crashed a bit when he landed.

Mum yelled down the stairs.

"What's going on, Joe? Be careful!"

"I need room to build up speed anyway," said Joe. "Let's go outside where Mum can't hear us."

It was fun – the best fun Joe had had since before his den was wrecked. They took turns and both got out of breath.

It was Joe's go. He took a big leap and landed hard. He fell sideways and crashed right into Dad's new flowerbed. He crawled out and turned round to look.

"Oh no!" he said. A lot of the plants were broken.

Mum chose that moment to look out of the window.

"JOE!" she called. "Are you all right?

Come in here!"

Joe got another telling-off.

"There's one thing, though," Mum finished. "If you're well enough to do that, you're well enough for school. Back you go on Monday."

Joe and Mike trailed upstairs again.

"What else can we do?" said Mike.

"Not a lot," said Joe. "I'm fed up of staying in. I can't wait till I can start on my new clubhouse." He stopped suddenly. He hadn't meant to tell Mike! The clubhouse was only for him himself, but it was too late!

"What clubhouse?" asked Mike.

So Joe had to tell him. He tried to make it sound not very interesting but Mike got more and more excited as Joe told him what Andy had said.

"That's great!" cried Mike. "Can I help? I could be in the club!"

Joe's heart sank. Of course, if you had a clubhouse you had to have a club. He hadn't thought about that.

He tried to talk about something else but Mike wasn't listening.

"I helped my dad build a garden shed at our old house," he said. "I know how to use the tools and everything. Dad's got quite a lot of wood left over. He might let us have it."

Joe remembered how all those nice planks of Andy's had been burned on that bonfire. Perhaps letting Mike help might be a good idea. But the clubhouse wouldn't be all his own any more. He wished he'd kept his silly mouth shut.

"I'll see what Andy says," he said reluctantly.

Next time Andy came round, Joe told him about it.

"Well,' said Andy, "I don't mind if Mike's careful where he walks – and you too, for that matter! I don't want my vegetables damaged!" He looked closely at Joe. "You don't look too happy though."

"I told him by mistake," said Joe.

"I wanted it to be just mine. Mike's okay, but he's not lived here long. It's not like he's a best friend."

"He might be a bit lonely if he's new here," said Andy. "It's always good to have room for new friends. Anyway, you could let him be a visitor. The clubhouse needn't belong to him like it does to you."

Joe looked at Andy. Andy was a new friend! He had made room for Joe in his allotment. He could have grown more vegetables on that patch he was giving to Joe. Perhaps Joe should make room for Mike. It would be all right if he was just a visitor.

The big day came. Joe had to borrow Dad's wheelbarrow to take everything down to the allotment. He covered it with a plastic sheet while he helped Andy dig over the place he wanted to plant potatoes. Then, together, they levelled a patch of ground in the corner of the allotment. There wasn't time to do much more that day, but Andy put Joe's things safely under cover. He took a piece of wood and wrote

on it in big letters. He nailed it to a stake and pushed it in to the ground right in front of the level patch. Joe ran to get some chocolate and cans of cola. They stood there in the fading light, munching together.

"Andy, I'm very glad you had room in your allotment for me to have this corner," said Joe. "There's just never any room at home."

"Oh, I've got lots of room for you, Joe," said Andy. "And Joe, do you know something? God has too."

Joe looked at Andy. Andy grinned. Joe grinned back. He was very tired but he felt like doing a war dance. He had, maybe, two new friends. Andy was one. He was beginning to think God was another. And, at last, at long last, he had a place he could call his own.

He couldn't wait to show Mike, either. Mike was coming tomorrow and Mum had promised to pack an enormous special feast for them all. She was going to buy them four different sorts of doughnuts. Joe couldn't think of a better way to begin clubhouse life.

If you've enjoyed this book
why not look out for these other Snapshots titles…

The Angel Tree Adventure

Anne Thorne

Matt is not sure whether he will like being in America.

"Hamburgers are great and the ice cream is wonderful. It's just that I'm not used to facing Unidentified Fried Objects for breakfast!"

Then he meets Kim and Luke who show him an Angel Tree and they all decide to get involved. But none of them expects it to turn into an adventure or to end up being on TV!

ISBN 1 85999 474 1

Friends! Who needs them?

Kay Kinnear

Matthew has loads of friends – Mo and Mary the white mice, Bizzy the gerbil, Hoppy the rabbit, Nick and Nellie the newts…

But he has to make some human friends fast to stop his parents sending him away to boarding school. Matthew's frantic efforts to find friends sometimes end in disaster – like when he meets Slick, Jelly and Zero.

ISBN 1 85999 441 5

Who invented SISTERS?

Eleanor Watkins

Jack's house seemed to be full of people – all of them were bigger than Jack and all of them were his sisters. Sometimes it seemed as though he had five mothers instead of one! Jack wondered if God had made a mistake when he put Jack into this family.

Jack's sisters boss him around but sometimes having sisters isn't so bad if you get into a real pickle.

ISBN 1 85999 545 4

You can buy these books at your local Christian bookshop, or online at www.scriptureunion.org.uk/publishing or call Mail Order direct on 01908 856006.